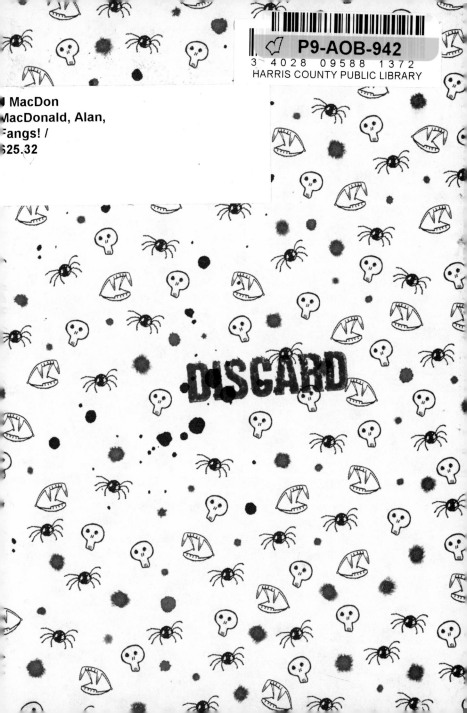

Dirty Bertie

Bertie

FANGS!

DAVID ROBERTS

WRITTEN BY ALAN MACDONALD

CAPSTONE

First published in the United States in 2012
by Stone Arch Books
A Capstone Imprint
1710 Roe Crest Drive
North Mankato, Minnesota 56003
www.capstonepub.com

First published by
Stripes Publishing
1 The Coda Centre, 189 Munster Road
London SW6 6AW

Library of Congress Cataloging-in-Publication Data is
available on the Library of Congress website.

ISBN: 978-1-4342-4601-1 (hardcover)
ISBN: 978-1-4342-4267-9 (paperback)

Summary: Bertie attempts to prove the grumpy school
janitor is a vampire, finds himself modeling the latest fashions,
and gets a serious "scare-cut" at the barbers.

Designer: Emily Harris

Photo Credits
Alan MacDonald, pg. 112 ; David Roberts, pg. 112

Printed in the United States of America in Stevens Point, Wisconsin.
042012   006678WZF12

TABLE OF CONTENTS

FANGS!

CHAPTER 1

It was Book Week at Bertie's school, and everyone, even the teachers, had come dressed as a character from their favorite book. Bertie looked around the playground. There were four witches, a sprinkling of fairies, and *a lot* of Harry Potters.

Bertie's friend Darren had come dressed as Dennis the Menace. Eugene, his other best friend, was dressed as Willy Wonka.

Bertie smiled to himself. His costume was better than anyone else's. He was Count Dracula. He wore a long black cloak and a pair of plastic fangs. A rubber bat dangled from his wrist like a yo-yo.

"Who are you supposed to be?" asked Eugene.

Bertie glared at his friend. "Who do you think?" he replied.

"I don't know," Eugene said, shrugging. "The Big Bad Wolf?"

"I'm Count Dracula!" said Bertie.

"Dracula doesn't wear tennis shoes," Darren pointed out.

Suddenly, a dark shadow fell over the boys. "Good morning!" a sinister voice said.

Bertie turned around and gasped. It was another vampire! Only this one was ten times taller and scarier than he was!

"Haha! Did I frighten you?" the vampire asked, taking out his fangs.

"Mr. Grouch!" Bertie exclaimed.

"That's Count Grouch to you," the

school's janitor corrected Bertie. "I see
you had the same idea. Spooky, huh?"
He looked down at something by Bertie's
foot. "What's that?"

"A candy wrapper," said Bertie.

"LITTER!" Mr. Grouch hollered. "Pick
it up!"

"But I didn't . . ." Bertie started to say.

"PICK IT UP!" Mr. Grouch repeated.
"And don't ever drop litter on my
playground. I have my eye on you." With
that, he put his fangs back in his mouth
and swept away, trailing his cape behind
him.

"Yikes!" Eugene said. "He scared me
to death!"

"Me too," Darren agreed. "How does
he sneak up on people like that?"

Bertie scowled. "I can't believe it. He stole my costume! Dracula was my idea!"

"Yeah, but his costume is better," said Darren. "I thought he really was a vampire."

"Maybe he is," Eugene suggested. Darren and Bertie stared at him.

"What do you mean?" Bertie asked.

"Well," said Eugene, "yesterday I walked past his shed. You know, the one out back that he always keeps locked? Mr. Grouch was sitting outside drinking something."

Darren shrugged. "So? What's so weird about that?" he asked.

"It's what he was drinking," Eugene said, looking nervous. "It looked like blood!"

"BLOOD?" gasped Bertie.

"Shh, not so loud!" Eugene hissed. "He'll hear you! And look at his costume. It fits perfectly. Maybe he really is a vampire."

"But vampires can't be outside in the daylight," Darren argued.

"Maybe he's some kind of half vampire," Bertie suggested. "Half vampire, half janitor."

The more he thought about it, the more the idea made sense.

Bertie had always thought there was something creepy about the school janitor. For one thing, he had small, beady eyes. And he hated children, especially Bertie. Plus, he had a weird habit of appearing out of nowhere, like a ghost.

"We have to stop him!" Bertie insisted.

"Stop him from doing what? He hasn't done anything yet," said Darren. "Except clean the bathrooms, I mean."

"How do you know?" said Bertie.

"He could be turning other teachers into vampires too! What about Miss Withers?"

Miss Withers used to be their science teacher. That is, until she went home sick one day and never returned. Or at least that's what people said.

But what if that wasn't the truth? What if the truth was that Mr. Grouch had turned her into a vampire?

Eugene looked nervous. "What should we do?" he asked.

"Spy on him," said Bertie. "We have to find out what he's up to. We can take turns."

"Good idea," said Darren. "You go first."

"ME? Why me?" Bertie asked.

"It was your idea," Darren said.
"Besides, he already hates you."

CHAPTER 2

Unfortunately, Bertie and his friends couldn't start their spying right away. They had to go to math class.

But Bertie wasn't about to let Mr. Grouch turn anyone into a vampire on his watch. He spent the rest of the morning in class keeping an eye on Mr.

Grouch through his classroom window.
He wrote down everything he saw in the
back of his math book.

Vampire Report

9:15 a.m. — Grouch sweeping up litter

10:00 a.m. — No vampires spotted

10:35 a.m. — Has cup of coffee and chocolate cookie

11:15 a.m. — Hasn't bitten anyone (yet)

During recess, Bertie hung around
the caretaker's shed, hoping to do some
spying. It wasn't long before Mr. Grouch
appeared, wearing his usual scowl. He
was still wearing his black vampire's
cape.

Bertie quickly ducked out of sight
behind the shed. Mr. Grouch unlocked

the door and went inside. A minute later,
he returned carrying a bag and a folding
chair. He sat down in the sunshine and
began to eat his lunch.

Bertie crept to the corner of the shed
and peered around. Mr. Grouch pulled
an old green Thermos out of his bag
and poured something bright red into a
plastic cup.

Bertie gasped.
BLOOD! Eugene was
right. There was no
escaping the horrible
truth. Mr. Grouch
was a vampire. He
had seen it with
his own eyes. Now
he just had to find proof. . . .

Bertie hurried back to the playground
and found Darren and Eugene waiting
for him. He quickly told his friends what
he'd seen.

"Blood?" said Darren, when Bertie had finished. "Are you sure?"

"Of course I'm sure! I saw him drink it!" said Bertie.

"So whose blood was it?" Darren asked.

"How am I supposed to know?" Bertie snapped.

"I told you he's a vampire!" said Eugene. "We should go to Miss Skinner!"

"Oh yeah, she's really going to believe us," said Darren.

Bertie shook his head. "First we need evidence. We have to prove he's really a vampire."

"How are we supposed to do that?" Eugene asked. "He's not drinking any of my blood!"

"Mine either," said Darren.

Bertie frowned, thinking hard. Where would Mr. Grouch hide something he wanted to keep secret?

"The shed!" cried Bertie. "I bet there's all kinds of stuff in there!"

"Like dead bodies!" said Darren.

"Or skeletons!" said Bertie.

Eugene turned pale. "But we're not allowed in there," he said. "Besides, Mr. Grouch always keeps the shed locked."

Bertie had forgotten that. Mr. Grouch kept the keys in his pocket and never let them out of his sight.

"We'll have to wait 'til he's busy," he said. "Then we'll borrow his keys and break into the shed. Piece of cake."

CHAPTER 3

After recess, Bertie and his friends found Mr. Grouch working in the boys' bathroom. A sign on the door read, "CLOSED FOR REPAIRS."

Bertie, Darren, and Eugene stood outside, whispering. "Here's the plan," Bertie told his friends. "You two keep him distracted, and I'll look for the keys."

Eugene looked nervous. "But what if he catches us?" he asked.

"Yeah. What if he tries to bite us and turn us into vampires too?" Darren added.

"He won't," said Bertie. "Not while there are teachers around."

It's now or never, Bertie thought. He quietly pushed open the door to the boys' bathroom, and the three of them crept inside.

Mr. Grouch was standing on a ladder fixing a light. He glared at the boys.

"Can't you read?" Mr. Grouch snapped. He pointed to the sign on the door.

"Oh, sorry!" said Bertie. "We, um . . . we just needed to use the bathroom."

"This one is closed," Mr. Grouch said. "You'll have to wait."

"Okay!" Eugene said quickly.

"Actually, I really have to go," Bertie said, glaring at his friend. "It's kind of an emergency. . . ."

"I SAID, COME BACK LATER!" roared Mr. Grouch.

Darren and Eugene gulped nervously and quickly backed toward the door.

Bertie followed more slowly. He could see Mr. Grouch's toolbox sitting on the floor near the door. On top was a set of silver keys. As he got closer, Bertie stumbled and pretended to trip over the toolbox.

CRASH!

"Watch where you're going!" Mr. Grouch yelled.

"Sorry!" Bertie said. He bent over and put away the tools that he'd spilled. Then he hurried back into the hallway to meet his friends.

"Well, that was a waste of time," said Darren.

"Not quite," Bertie said with a smile. He held up his hand, dangling the heavy ring of keys back and forth.

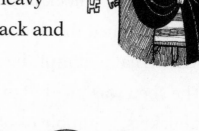

Mr. Grouch's shed stood by itself in a corner of the playground. It was strictly off limits to students. But that didn't stop Bertie. He stood in front of the shed and fiddled with the keys, trying to find the right one.

"Hurry up!" Eugene whispered. "What if someone comes?"

"I'm going as fast as I can!" Bertie hissed back. At last, he tried a small silver key. It turned in the lock with a click, and the padlock popped open.

Bertie opened the door and stepped inside. "What a dump!" he said.

The shed was piled high with boxes and buckets. A jumble of old paint cans littered the floor. Mr. Grouch's collection of brooms, rakes, and mops decorated the walls.

Darren looked around. "There's nothing here!"

"Okay, we've seen it, let's go!" begged Eugene.

"Wait a minute. There has to be something," said Bertie. "We have to find proof that Mr. Grouch is a vampire."

27

Eugene sighed, but stood by the door
to act as a lookout while the other two
searched.

Bertie found Mr. Grouch's dirty
overalls hanging on a hook. His bag
hung next to them. Inside, he found
a newspaper, some gardening gloves,
a lunch box . . . and Mr. Grouch's old
green Thermos.

"Look what I found!" Bertie
whispered excitedly.

"Open it," said Darren.

Bertie unscrewed the lid. The
Thermos was empty, but the inside
was smeared with bright red stains. He
sniffed it. The scent was familiar, but he
couldn't quite place it.

"Well?" asked Darren.

"Blood," Bertie said, nodding. "There's our proof!"

Eugene suddenly yelped. A tall, dark figure in a billowing cloak was marching across the playground toward the caretaker's shed.

"IT'S MR. GROUCH!" cried Eugene. "RUN!"

Darren and Eugene bolted out the door. Bertie looked around in a panic. He stuffed everything back into Mr. Grouch's bag, but kept the Thermos as evidence.

He ran to the door, but just as he reached it, a dark figure blocked his path.

"What do you think you're doing?" Mr. Grouch growled at him. His eyes blazed like fire. "Are you the one who stole my keys?"

"N-n-no," stammered Bertie.

"Liar! Hand 'em over!"

"You're too late," Bertie hollered. "I know the truth! I found proof!"

"Proof?" Mr. Grouch repeated. "Proof of what?"

"That you're a vampire!" said Bertie.

"A vampire? Don't be ridiculous!" cried Mr. Grouch. "Give me those keys. I'm not going to ask you again."

Mr. Grouch took a step closer. Bertie could see his deadly fangs sticking out of his mouth.

This is it, Bertie thought. *I'm going to be fanged to death! I have to escape!*

"YEEEARGHHHHH!" Bertie yelled

as he rushed at the vampire, knocking
him off balance. Mr. Grouch stepped
back into a paint can and promptly fell
over.

Bertie burst out of the shed door and
slammed it shut behind him.

CLICK! He snapped the padlock on the door closed and ran for his life.

"HEY!" Mr. Grouch yelled from inside the shed. "LET ME OUT!"

CHAPTER 4

Safely back in his classroom, Bertie stared out the window. Loud noises were coming from inside the shed across the playground.

THUMP! THUMP! BANG!

Mr. Grouch had been locked in the shed for an hour, and he did NOT sound happy. Luckily, Miss Boot, who was currently dressed as some kind of witch, was too busy going on and on about homework to pay attention.

Someone suddenly poked Bertie in the back.

"What if he gets out of the shed?" hissed Eugene.

"He can't!" Bertie hissed back.

"But what if he does?" Eugene said. "He saw you, Bertie!"

THUMP! Bertie looked around. Was it his imagination, or were the noises getting louder?

THUMP! BANG! CLUNK!

Mr. Grouch was trying to break the door down. Bertie gulped. Maybe vampires were stronger than he'd thought.

"BERTIE!" Miss Boot hollered. "Stop staring out the window! Get to work!"

Bertie tried to concentrate. He looked down at what he'd scribbled in his science book.

THE EARTH GOES AROUND THE SUN.
THE SUN IS BIG AND RED.
LIKE BLOOD . . .

Bertie glanced up and looked out the window again. ARGH! The shed door was open and hanging off its hinges. Mr. Grouch had escaped!

Bertie's heart beat faster. *Don't panic*, he thought. *Miss Boot is here.*

*Even vampires are probably afraid of
her. Besides, he won't come into the
classroom. . . .*

WHAM!

The door to the classroom burst
open. Mr. Grouch stood there, red-faced
and furious. His cape was torn, and his
pants were covered with paint splatters.
Eugene let out a scream.

"Mr. Grouch!" cried Miss Boot. "What
on earth are you doing?"

The janitor stormed into the room. "Where is that boy?" he panted. "Just wait 'til I get my hands on him!"

Bertie tried to quietly slide down under his desk. But Mr. Grouch spotted him.

"YOU!" he yelled, pointing at Bertie. "I want a word with you!"

Miss Boot stepped in front of him, blocking his way. "Mr. Grouch! You are interrupting my class! What is this about?"

"Ask him!" said Mr. Grouch, pointing at Bertie. "He stole my keys. He locked me in the shed!"

Miss Boot glared at him. "BERTIE!" she said. "Is that true?"

"I had to," Bertie said. "He's a vampire!"

Mr. Grouch rolled his eyes. "I'm not a vampire! It's a costume for Book Week!"

"Don't listen to him!" said Bertie, desperately. "He drinks blood! I saw him!"

"BLOOD?" said Mr. Grouch. "What are you talking about?"

"This," said Bertie. He reached under his desk and pulled out the Thermos he'd stolen from Mr. Grouch's bag. He held it up to show everyone the inside.

"See? RED! Those are bloodstains!"

Mr. Grouch snorted. "That's tomato soup!"

"W-what?" Bertie stuttered.

"Soup!" Mr. Grouch repeated, rolling his eyes. "Tomato soup. I had it for lunch."

"Not . . . blood?" Bertie said. He sniffed the Thermos. Now he realized why that smell was so familiar.

Oops! Bertie thought. If it wasn't blood, then that meant Mr. Grouch wasn't really a vampire. He was just a furious janitor Bertie had locked in a shed for an hour.

Bertie backed away slowly. There was only one thing to do. . . .

"BERTIE!" yelled Miss Boot. "COME BACK HERE!"

CHAPTER 1

Bertie hunched over his breakfast cereal, his hair flopping in his eyes.

SLURP! MUNCH! CRUNCH!

Bertie's mom looked up from her breakfast. "BERTIE!" she said with a sigh.

"What?" he asked.

"Your hair!" his mom exclaimed.

"What do you mean? What's wrong with it?" Bertie asked.

"It's a mess!"

Bertie shrugged and shook his hair out of his eyes. "It looks okay to me," he said.

"I'm surprised you can see anything at all," his mom told him. "You need a haircut!"

"NOOO!" he cried.

Bertie absolutely HATED having his hair cut. He liked it just the way it was. Scruffy. Messy. Dirty. Bertie never combed his hair or brushed it. And he complained whenever his mom made him wash it.

As for haircuts — ugh, why bother? His parents were always talking about saving money. If he gave up haircuts, it would probably save them thousands of dollars. They should be grateful. They should be giving him a bigger allowance instead of complaining!

Dad looked at Mom. "Are you going to take him?" he asked.

"No way," said Mom. "It's your turn."

"It's not!" Dad exclaimed.

"Of course it is!" Mom insisted. "I took him last time, remember?"

Mom wasn't likely to forget. Bertie had had lice at the time, which they only discovered when the hairdresser screamed. They hadn't been back there since.

"And besides," Mom added, "I won't be home in time."

Dad groaned. "Okay, fine. I'll take him after school."

Bertie looked horrified. "I can't!" he argued. "I . . . I'll have homework!"

"That never stops you from watching TV," Dad said. "We'll go to Bob's Barbershop at the mall."

Bertie almost choked on his cereal. Not Bob's Barbershop! His friend

Darren had gone there
once, and he'd come
back looking like a
hedgehog! Everyone
had called him Spike
for weeks!

"Not there!" said
Bertie. "I don't want
to go to Bob's!"

"It's fine, Bertie,"
said Dad. "What's the big deal? Lots of
people get their hair cut there."

"You don't!" said Bertie.

"No, well, I get my hair cut at Super
Snips," said Dad. "It's just, um . . .
easier."

Super Snips was the new hair salon
in town. Bertie's other friend Eugene

went there with his mom. They had comfy chairs to sit in, and comics to read, and they handed out free lollipops. The only thing Bob's Barbershop handed out was terrible haircuts.

"Why can't I go to Super Snips?" asked Bertie.

"Too fancy," said Mom.

"Too expensive," said Dad.

"I don't see why you're making such a big deal about it, Bertie," said Mom. "Dad could use a haircut too. Why don't you both go together?"

"No, thanks," Dad said quickly. "Mine can wait."

"So can mine," said Bertie, reaching up to touch his head. "In fact, I think my hair has stopped growing!"

Mom gave him a look. "Bertie, you are getting a haircut, and that's final," she said.

Bertie sighed heavily and stomped upstairs. He went into the bathroom and looked at his reflection in the mirror. What was wrong with his hair, anyway? He liked it getting in his eyes.

Too bad I wasn't born before haircuts were invented, Bertie thought. *Cavemen used to walk around looking like hairy apes. I would have made a great caveman.*

Bertie stared at himself, trying to imagine what he would look like without any hair. Darren would laugh his socks off. They'd call him "Bald Bertie" at school. He'd have to wear a bag over his head. Then he *really* wouldn't be able to see anything.

CHAPTER 2

After school, Bertie invited Eugene to come over to his house to play. Dad was in the kitchen working on his computer when they walked in.

"Dad!" said Bertie. "Can Eugene come over and play?"

"Not today," Dad said. "I'm taking you to get your hair cut, remember?"

Bertie groaned. He was hoping that having Eugene over would give him an excuse to stay at home.

"But Eugene's already here," he said.

"I can see that," his dad said.

"Hi, Mr. Burns!" Eugene called.

"Can't he stay? Just for a little while?" Bertie begged.

"My mom already said it was okay," Eugene added.

Dad looked at his watch and sighed. "All right!" he agreed. "But only for half an hour. The barbershop closes at five o'clock."

Eugene and Bertie turned and ran upstairs before Dad could change his mind. Bertie slammed the door to his room behind them.

"What's wrong?" Eugene asked.

"Didn't you hear?" Bertie said. "I have to go get my hair cut."

"So?" Eugene said. "What's so bad about that?"

"It's *where* I have to go get it cut," said Bertie. "Bob's Barbershop."

Eugene looked at him. "Haha!" he laughed. "I can't wait to see you tomorrow!"

"It's not funny," Bertie groaned.

"Why don't you go to Super Snips instead?" Eugene suggested.

"I already tried that," said Bertie. "Dad won't take me. You have to help me."

Bertie racked his brains. There had to be something he could do. Just then,

his eyes fell on the kitchen scissors he'd
borrowed to cut out some dinosaur
pictures. Of course! Mom and Dad
wanted him to get a haircut, so why not
get one? He could cut it himself!

Wait a minute, Bertie thought. *Maybe that's not such a great plan.*

It would be impossible to see what he was doing. It would be much safer to get someone else to do it. Luckily, Bertie knew just the right person.

"Eugene," said Bertie. "I've got a great idea. . . ."

Five minutes later, Bertie sat in a chair with a towel draped around his shoulders.

"Are you sure about this?" Eugene asked hesitantly.

"Of course I'm sure!" Bertie replied. "I told you, it's fine!"

"But what if I get in trouble?" Eugene asked, sounding worried. "If your dad finds out what we're doing, he's going to be really mad!"

"No, he won't," said Bertie. "He wants me to get my hair cut!"

"Yeah, but not by me!" Eugene protested. "I've never done this before!"

"It's easy!" said Bertie. "It's just like

cutting paper. Now hurry up and do it before someone comes!"

Eugene took a deep breath. He had a bad feeling about this. He chose a long piece of hair sticking up on the back of Bertie's head.

SNIP!

"There. All done," Eugene said.

Bertie rolled his eyes. "You haven't even started yet!"

"Yes, I have!" said Eugene. "You said cut your hair. I cut this one!"

"You have to do it all or no one will notice I got it cut," Bertie said.

"How much shorter?" Eugene asked.

"I don't know! Short enough that it's not in my eyes and sticking up everywhere."

Eugene sighed heavily. He grabbed a clump of Bertie's hair in one hand and raised the scissors with the other.

SNIP! SNIP! SNIP!

CHAPTER 3

Bertie closed his eyes as pieces of hair fell to the floor. He didn't know why he'd never thought of this before. Why bother going to the hair salon at all when you could get a perfectly good haircut at home?

The more he thought about it, the

better the idea seemed. He and Eugene could set up their own business. Eugene could cut the hair while Bertie took the money. People would be lining up around the block. Girls would have to pay double, obviously, because they had more hair.

SNIP! SNIP! SNIP!

Eugene stopped to rest for a second. Once you got started, cutting hair was easy. You just had to chop away at it like his dad did when he trimmed the bushes. He stepped back for a minute to admire his handiwork.

"Well?" asked Bertie. "How does it look?"

"Uh . . . good," said Eugene. "Yeah, it looks good."

"Is it shorter?" Bertie asked.

"Oh, yeah. It's definitely shorter," Eugene said.

Bertie stood up and shook off the towel. There was a pretty big pile of his hair on the floor. He went over to take a look in the mirror.

"ARGHHHHHHHHHHH!" Bertie screamed. He looked crazy! Patches of his hair were missing, and the pieces that were left stuck out in every direction.

"What did you do?" he asked Eugene.

"What do you mean?" Eugene said. "You asked me to cut it!"

"Not like this!" Bertie said. "I look like an ALIEN!"

"It's not my fault!" Eugene hollered.

Dirty Bertie

62

"I've never cut anyone's hair before. You said you wanted it shorter!"

"I meant shorter all over!" said Bertie. He turned back to the mirror. "What am I going to do?"

Eugene sat down on the ground. "It's not that bad. It'll probably grow back in a few weeks."

"A FEW WEEKS!" yelled Bertie. This was terrible. He should have known better than to trust Eugene. What were his parents going to say when they saw his hair? Dad would be furious. Mom would probably faint.

"BERTIE!" Dad called from downstairs. "Time to go!"

"Um . . . just a minute!" Bertie shouted.

Eugene stared at him in panic. "What do we do?"

"Bertie! Hurry up!" yelled Dad.

Bertie looked around in desperation. They had to hide the evidence. He stuffed the towel and scissors into one of the drawers and slammed it shut. He glanced at the floor, which was covered with all the hair that used to be on his head. Bertie swept it up and looked around for someplace to hide it.

THUMP! THUMP! THUMP! Dad was coming up the stairs.

Bertie stuffed the hair into his pocket. right as the door swung open.

"Come on," said Dad. "We need to — ARGH! WHAT DID YOU DO TO YOUR HAIR?"

"This?" Bertie said, pointing at his
head. "Eugene did it."

"It wasn't my fault! He made me!"
Eugene cried.

Bertie shrugged. "You said I needed a haircut, so I got one."

"I meant at the barbershop, not one you gave yourself!" Dad said. He looked down and checked his watch. "Come on, we're barely going to make it. We'll drop Eugene off at his house on the way."

"Where are we going?" asked Bertie.

"To the barbershop, where else?" Dad said.

"But . . . but I already got a haircut!" Bertie protested.

"Yes," said Dad, "and now you have to get another one before your mother gets home!"

CHAPTER 4

Bob's Barbershop didn't have free lollipops or comics to read. It had three black leather chairs and one barber — Bob. Bob had been cutting hair the exact same way for twenty years.

"Who's next?" Bob growled.

Bertie glanced around the room.

There were only three people waiting: him, Dad, and a nervous-looking freckle-faced boy.

Bertie looked at the other boy. "After you," he offered.

"No, you go ahead," said the boy, looking terrified.

"No, no, you go," Bertie said. "I insist. You were here first."

The boy hung his head and plodded over to where Bob the barber was waiting.

Bertie thought Bob looked more like a boxer than a barber. He had a thick neck like a bulldog and razor-short gray hair. His muscular arms were covered in tattoos.

"So, what'll it be?" Bob asked as his victim sat down.

"Um . . . just a trim, please," squeaked the boy.

Bob reached for his Number One electric clippers. "Short back and sides," he said.

BUZZ, BUZZ, BUZZ!

The clippers hummed. Chunks of red hair fell to the floor.

BUZZ, BUZZ, BUZZ!

Bertie shifted nervously in his seat.

He glanced at the door, praying for another customer to arrive. He'd rather have patchy, sticking-up hair for the rest of his life than face Bob and his electric clippers.

The clippers stopped buzzing. The freckle-faced boy climbed down from the chair, rubbing his neck. He looked like a shaved coconut.

Bertie kept his eyes on the floor as the boy hurried out, looking embarrassed.

Now there was no one else in line. There was no escape.

Dad was reading the newspaper. Bob swept up the hair on the floor. He set down the broom and cracked his knuckles loudly.

This is it, thought Bertie. *Goodbye, hair.*

"Who's next?" Bob grunted, looking over at Bertie.

Bertie lost his nerve and pointed at his dad. "He is!"

Dad looked up from his newspaper. "What?" he said.

"Take a seat," Bob instructed.

"No, no, I'm, uh, just waiting," Dad stammered.

"Then it's your turn," said Bob. "Take a seat."

Dad frantically looked around the

room for an escape. "Bertie," he pleaded. "You go."

Bertie shook his head. "That's okay. You go ahead. Mom said you needed a haircut too."

"Yes, but not . . ." Dad started to say.

"Hurry up," Bob snapped. "I'm closing in five minutes."

Dad glared at Bertie as he walked slowly over to the chair and sat down heavily. Bob draped a towel around his neck.

"What'll it be?" Bob asked.

"Uh . . . just a very, very light trim, please," said Dad.

Bob switched on his Number One clippers.

"Short back and sides," he said.

BUZZ, BUZZ, BUZZ . . .

Mom was setting the table for dinner when the front door slammed.

"Is that you, Bertie?" she called. "How did your haircut go? Please tell me you behaved yourself this time."

"It went fine!" Bertie said as he walked into the kitchen.

Mom stared at Bertie's head in horror. "What happened to your hair?" she exclaimed.

"Eugene cut it," Bertie told her
cheerfully.

"What?" cried Mom. "I thought Dad
was taking you to the barbershop!"

"He did, but Bob didn't have time to
cut my hair," Bertie said.

"What? Then whose hair did he cut?"
Mom asked.

Bertie grinned and turned toward the door. Dad walked in with a bright red face.

"ARGHHHHHH!" screamed Mom. "What happened?"

"It's okay," said Bertie. "It'll probably grow back in a few weeks!"

FASHION!

CHAPTER 1

Bertie loved Saturday mornings. Saturdays were for watching TV, seeing his friends, or taking his dog to the park.

But not today. Today he had to go shopping with his mom. Bertie hated shopping more than anything. The stores Mom dragged him to never had anything he was interested in. It was the absolute worst.

This particular Saturday, his mom had dragged him to Dibble's Department Store to buy new school shoes.

"Remember, Bertie," Mom said as they walked into the store, "don't touch anything, and DON'T go wandering off."

"I won't!" Bertie said with a sigh. Where did she think he would wander off to, anyway — to look at bath mats?

Mom studied the map of the store. The shoe department was on the second floor.

"Can we take the elevator?" begged Bertie. "Please!"

"I suppose," said Mom, stopping to look at a perfume that was on sale.

Bertie ran ahead and pressed the button for the elevator. He loved riding the elevator. He didn't know why his parents hadn't thought of installing one at home. It would save so much time when he needed to get from his room to the kitchen!

He pressed the button again and held it down.

DING! The elevator finally arrived. The doors slid open and several people got out. Bertie stepped inside, happy to have the elevator all to himself.

Suddenly he realized something. *Wait a minute*, Bertie thought. *Where's Mom?* The doors were starting to close! He spotted her standing at the perfume counter.

"Mom!" shouted Bertie.

"Bertie, wait!" Mom yelled, running over.

But it was too late. The elevator doors shut in her face. Bertie blinked. He pushed the buttons on the wall. But instead of the doors opening, the elevator started to go up.

Uh-oh, Bertie thought. *I'm in big trouble. Mom is going to be furious!*

He pressed all the buttons at once, but the elevator didn't listen. It just kept rising.

Finally the elevator stopped with a jolt. *PING!* The doors slid open, and Bertie stepped out. He didn't recognize this floor at all. But before he could change his mind, the elevator was already gone.

Now what? Bertie thought, glancing around. His mom would expect him to go back to where he'd gotten lost. That meant the ground floor.

Maybe it'll be faster to take the stairs, he thought. Bertie set off, wandering past row after row of beds. He kept his eyes peeled, looking for a sign to point him in the right direction.

Five minutes later, Bertie was still wandering. Turning a corner, he saw a large room crowded with people. Rows of chairs were facing a long stage.

Maybe someone famous is coming, Bertie thought. He was about to ask for help when a woman wearing a nametag that read "LAURA" appeared.

"Oh, thank goodness! There you are!" she said.

Bertie felt a wave of relief. Mom must have sent someone to find him. Laura glanced at her clipboard. "It's Bernie, isn't it?" she said.

"Uh . . . it's Bertie actually," Bertie corrected her.

"Oh, sorry. Bertie," Laura said, checking her list. "It was probably just a typo. Anyway, you're here now. Hurry up, everyone is waiting."

Bertie looked confused. "Um . . . I'm just looking for my mom," he said.

"Don't worry," said Laura. "She called. She's on her way."

"She is?" Bertie asked.

"Yes, she said she'll meet you here," Laura replied.

Phew! Bertie thought. *At least I'm not in trouble.*

Laura opened a door and ushered him through. "Claudia's been going crazy!" she said. "We thought you weren't coming."

Bertie looked around the room. It looked like some kind of changing room. A man was pulling on a shirt. Another hurried by in his underwear.

This definitely isn't the shoe department, Bertie thought.

CHAPTER 2

"He's here!" yelled Laura, above the noise. "Claudia, I found him!"

"Oh, thank goodness!" Claudia replied. She looked down her nose at Bertie. "You're sure this is the right one?"

"Yes, this is Bertie," Laura said. "I found him outside."

Claudia sighed. "Well, try to do something with his hair. I'll be there in a moment."

Bertie frowned. "But I'm just here for new—" he started to say.

Before he could finish, someone pushed him into a chair. A group of women swooped down on him and got to work. One combed his hair, another dabbed something on his face, and a third scolded him for his dirty nails. They all talked at once.

"Head up!"

"Hold still!"

"Look at me, not over there!"

"I need to find my mom," said Bertie, squirming to escape. "She's supposed to meet me here."

"I'm sure she's out front, waiting to see you," one of the women said.

"Is this going to take long?" Bertie asked. "I'm supposed to be getting shoes."

"Don't worry, Claudia will take care of that," one of the women replied. "Look up for me!"

Bertie looked up.

"There!" said the lady. "All done."

Bertie swiveled his chair to look at himself in the mirror. He gasped. He was wearing makeup! His hair stuck up in the air, and he had pink stuff all over

his face. He tried to wipe it off with the back of his hand.

Claudia came over to inspect him. "Well," she said with a sigh. "I suppose he'll have to do. Where are his clothes?"

"I'm wearing them," said Bertie.

"Not those! They're terrible!" Claudia exclaimed. She checked her list. "He should be in sportswear."

Bertie looked down at his clothes. They seemed okay to him. True, his sweater had something spilled on it, but that was normal. And he was wearing his best jeans. They were practically clean!

Claudia was busy sorting through shirts and jackets hanging on a rack. She grabbed a bright yellow sweatshirt with the word DAZZLE written across the front and handed it to Bertie.

"Put this on," she commanded.

"Who? Me?" asked Bertie.

"Of course you!" Claudia replied. "Who else?"

"But I just want new shoes!" Bertie said.

Claudia snapped her fingers. "Someone bring him some sneakers!" she called. "And hurry! We're on in five minutes!"

The assistants swooped down again.

They hurried Bertie into the sweatshirt and zipped it up to hide his clothes. It was way too big and a horrible bright yellow color. Bertie thought he looked like a big fat banana.

"Perfect!" one of the assistants said. "Now let's get these tennis shoes on."

Bertie stared. "I'm not wearing those!" he cried.

The assistant glanced at the clock.

"Okay, fine. We don't have time for a tantrum. Keep your own."

"Excuse me," said Bertie loudly. "Has anyone seen my mom?"

But no one listened. The music next door had fallen silent, and an air of anticipation swept through the room. Claudia climbed onto a chair and clapped her hands. "We're starting!" she cried. "Places, people, places!"

Everyone started rushing around like a fire alarm had gone off. Bertie found himself herded into a line of people in a long hallway. They were all wearing bright Dazzle clothing like him. Up ahead, a set of steps led to a curtained stage.

Claudia clapped her hands again to

Dirty Bertie

get everyone's attention. "Remember, everyone, you are graceful swans, not ducklings! Good luck!" She blew them all kisses.

The music started up again, and the first person stepped through the curtain and onto the stage. Bertie caught a glimpse of rows of people on the other side.

Where is my mom? Bertie thought frantically.

CHAPTER 3

Down on the ground floor, Mom was starting to worry. This wasn't the first time Bertie had gotten lost, but in the past he'd always turned up, looking muddy and messy or clutching a caterpillar.

This time, however, there was no sign

of him. Dibble's was a huge store, and Bertie could be anywhere.

After a few more minutes passed with no sign of Bertie, Mom hurried to the Help Desk and explained the situation to the woman working there.

"And what does he look like?" the woman asked.

Mom thought. "Small," she said. "With scruffy hair and dirty jeans. Probably a runny nose."

"Runny nose . . ." the woman repeated, writing it all down. Mom wished she would write a bit faster. "And what's his name?"

"Bertie," said Mom. "It's my fault. I never should have taken my eyes off him."

The assistant smiled. "I'm sure he can't have gotten very far," she said. "I'll make an announcement over the speaker system."

She pushed a button and spoke into a microphone. Her voice carried through

the store. "Will Bertie please come to the Help Desk on the ground floor? His mother is waiting for him — with a tissue."

Up on the fourth floor, the music was so loud that Bertie didn't hear a word of the announcement. Every now and then, someone at the front of the line went up the steps and disappeared through the curtain. Bursts of applause came from the other side of the curtain. Bertie wondered if someone famous had arrived.

Everyone else in the line was

grabbing stuff from a box of footballs, tennis rackets, and other sports equipment. Bertie grabbed a skateboard from the box as he neared the front of the line.

Suddenly, a door burst open, and a shaggy-haired boy rushed into the room.

"Hi!" he panted. "I'm Bernie."

"That's funny," said Bertie. "I'm Bertie."

"Are you in the show too?" Bernie asked. "Where's Laura? I'm not too late, am I?"

"Don't ask me," said Bertie. "Everyone here is nuts! Late for what?"

"The fashion show, duh," Bernie said. "I'm a model, same as you."

"A model? Haha!" Bertie laughed. You'd never catch him prancing up and down a runway in stupid clothes!

Hang on a minute . . . he was wearing stupid clothes . . . and makeup!

Suddenly, the horrible truth dawned on him. This was a fashion show, and he was in it!

ARGHHH! Bertie thought.

"Bertie! You're next!" Claudia hissed, grabbing him by the arm.

"But I . . ." Bertie tried to say. But it was too late. Claudia pushed him through the curtain and onto the runway.

CHAPTER 4

Bertie was immediately blinded by
the bright spotlights. He could feel the
audience staring at him. This was a
nightmare! There'd obviously been some
terrible mistake. That other boy, Bernie,
should have been standing up here, not
him!

Bertie desperately looked around for some way to escape. He could see Claudia glaring at him from behind the curtain. She waved him forward on the runway toward where the other models were striking poses.

Bertie gulped. No way was he doing that. It was time for a speedy exit. He set the skateboard down, scooted a few steps, and pushed off hard.

ZOOOOOOM!

Bertie whizzed down the stage, past rows of surprised faces. The audience clapped, thinking it was all part of the show. Bertie looked up and gasped. The other models had turned around and were headed back down the runway. He was heading straight for them!

"Out of the way!" he yelled. "I can't stop!"

CRASH!

Bertie plowed right into them. The models flew into the audience. A soccer ball bounced off a woman sitting in the front row.

Bertie sat up and rubbed his head. Luckily, he seemed to be okay. But some of the models were climbing back onto the stage, and they did not look happy. Bertie glanced around and saw Claudia walking toward him.

Bertie gulped. He was trapped! Or maybe not . . .

Without a second thought, Bertie
jumped off the stage and took off
running through the audience.

Five minutes later, Bertie reached the
ground floor and stopped to catch his
breath. Luckily, no one seemed to be
following him. He unzipped the
yellow sweatshirt and stuffed it
into a nearby trashcan.

"THERE YOU ARE, BERTIE!" someone yelled.

It was Mom! Never in his life had Bertie been so glad to see his mom.

"Where on earth have you been?" Mom asked as she hugged him in relief.

"Oh, um, nowhere special," Bertie said. "I was looking for you."

He decided it was probably better not to mention what had happened upstairs with Claudia. Mom would just get mad.

"Didn't you hear the announcement?" she said. "They called your name over the speaker system!"

Bertie shook his head. He hadn't heard anything.

"What's that on your face?" Mom asked suddenly. "Is that . . . makeup?"

Bertie's face turned red. He'd forgotten all about the makeup.

"Uh, yeah," he said. "I got bored waiting, so I was just . . . um . . . trying it on."

Mom frowned, but didn't ask any more questions. She was just grateful to have found Bertie safe and sound.

"Next time, wait for me before you get in the elevator," she scolded him. "Now, let's go see if we can find you some shoes."

This time, Mom and Bertie took the stairs together. When they reached the second floor, Mom stopped to read a poster.

"Look at this, Bertie!" she said.
"They're holding a fashion show!
How fun! Why don't we go . . . Bertie?
Bertie?"

Mom looked around. But Bertie had
disappeared again.

When he was young, **Alan MacDonald** dreamed of becoming a professional soccer player, but when he  won a pen in a writing competition, his fate was sealed. Alan is now a successful author and television writer and has written several award-winning children's books, which have been translated into many languages.

David Roberts worked as a fashion illustrator in Hong Kong before turning to children's books. He has worked with a long list of  writers, including Philip Ardagh, Georgia Byng, Carol Ann Duffy, and Chris Priestley. David has also won a gold award in the Nestle Children's Book Prize for *Mouse Noses On Toast* in 2006, and was shortlisted for the 2010 CILIP Kate Greenaway medal for *The Dunderheads*.

Read more about Bertie at
capstonekids.com/characters/dirty-bertie